The Sugar Ball

READ ALL THE CANDY FAIRIES BOOKS!

Chocolate Dreams

Rainbow Swirl

Caramel Moon

Cool Mint

Magic Hearts

COMING SOON:

A Valentine's Surprise

Bubble Gum Rescue

Candy Fairies

The Sugar Ball

HELEN PERELMAN

ILLUSTRATED BY
ERICA-JANE WATERS

SIMON AND SCHUSTER

First published in Great Britain in 2013 by Simon & Schuster UK Ltd
A CBS COMPANY

Published in the USA in 2011 by Aladdin,
an imprint of Simon & Schuster Children's Division, New York.

1 3 5 7 9 10 8 6 4 2

Simon & Schuster UK Ltd
1st Floor
222 Gray's Inn Road
London
WC1X 8HB

www.simonandschuster.co.uk
www.simonandschuster.com.au

Simon & Schuster Australia, Sydney
Simon & Schuster India, New Delhi

A CIP catalogue copy for this book is available from the British Library.

ISBN: 978-1-4711-1980-4
Ebook ISBN: 978-1-4711-1981-1

Printed and bound by CPI Group (UK) Ltd, Croydon, CR0 4YY

For Karli and Hana Grace Meyer

Contents

The Sugar Ball

CHAPTER
1

Sweet Thoughts

Cocoa smiled as she flew across Chocolate Woods. The sun was shining and the air was full of sweet, rich chocolate scents. The Chocolate Fairy spread her golden wings and glided down to Chocolate Falls. *Yum*, thought Cocoa as she licked her lips. There was nothing better than fresh milk chocolate.

"Cocoa!" Melli, the Caramel Fairy, called. "Over here!" Melli was sitting underneath a chocolate oak tree. She waved to get Cocoa's attention.

Waving back, Cocoa fluttered down to her friend's side. Melli was always on time – or early. She was a shy fairy, but her sweet caramel nature was part of what kept their group of friends sticking together – no matter what.

"What a *choc-o-rific* day!" Cocoa sang. She smiled at her friend.

"Only one more week until the Sugar Ball," Melli burst out. "I can't wait!" She took out a light caramel twist from her bag. "What do you think? I just had to show you right away." She held up the long caramel rope for Cocoa to view.

"It looks delicious," Cocoa commented.

"Won't this be perfect for the sash on my dress?" Melli asked. "I've been searching for just the right size trim."

Cocoa laughed. All any of her friends could think about was the Sugar Ball at Candy Castle and the dresses they'd wear to the party. The big ball was the grandest – and sweetest – of the season. The Sugar Ball was a celebration of the sugar harvest. Fairies from all over came to the Royal Gardens for the party. Princess Lolli, the ruling fairy princess, always made the party the most scrumptious of the year.

"I think that will be the perfect addition to your outfit," Cocoa said. She touched the golden caramel twist. "This is the exact right colour for your dress."

Melli clapped her hands. "I knew you'd say that!" she said, grinning. "Cara wanted me to make her one just like this too."

Cara was Melli's little sister and always wanted to be just like her big sister.

"Did you help her?" Cocoa asked.

"Sure as sugar," Melli said. "She's so excited about her first ball." She stopped and admired her dress. "Now I just need to find the right necklace."

"You should ask Berry to make you one of her sparkly fruit-chew necklaces," Cocoa said. She was used to her friend Berry, the Fruit Fairy, always talking about fashion, but this year all her friends were concerned about their Sugar Ball dresses and jewellery. Everyone wanted to make her ball gown special and unique. Even Cocoa!

"You're right," Melli said. "I should ask Berry. I just hope she doesn't say she's too busy. Did you know that she is weaving the material for her dress herself? Her dress is going to be *sweet-tacular*!"

"Hmm," Cocoa muttered. She was actually growing a little tired of all the talk about dresses. Even though she wanted to look her best, she had another idea of how to make her entrance at the ball special.

"Do you think Char will remember me?" Melli asked, interrupting Cocoa's thoughts. Her light brown eyes had a faraway gaze. Like most fairies in Sugar Valley, she loved the Sugar Pops. They were brothers who played in a band together and sang the sweetest songs. Char was the lead singer in the band and Melli's supersweet crush.

"How could they forget you?" Cocoa asked. "You were the Candy Fairy who saved Caramel Moon!" In the fall, when the candy corn crop was in danger, Melli was the one who discovered the problem. Together with their fairy friends, they saved the Caramel Moon festival, where the Sugar Pops played. They even got to meet Carob, Chip, and Char! Seeing them again at the Sugar Ball would definitely sugarcoat the night.

"I know it's just a rumor that they'll come," Melli said, "but I hope the sugar fly buzz is right. I would love to see them again." Melli clasped her hands together and put them under her chin. She looked over at Cocoa. "What's in your bag?"

Looking down at her bag, Cocoa smiled. There were a couple of strands of marshmallow threads sticking out of her chocolate weave bag. "I was down at Marshmallow Marsh this morning," she explained.

"What are you doing with marshmallow?" Melli asked. "You can't use that for your dress. Marshmallow is too sticky to work for an outfit."

Cocoa laughed. "No, not for my dress," she said. "Something else for the ball." She sat down and took out a sheet of paper from her pocket. "Last week when Raina was reading from the Fairy Code Book, there was that story about the princess and her chocolate sceptre. Do you remember?"

Raina, the Gummy Fairy, was their good friend, who loved to read. She had nearly memorized the entire Fairy Code Book!

Nodding, Melli thought back to the story. "It was a magic sceptre made of the finest sugar. The picture in the book showed a beautiful chocolate wand."

"Yes," Cocoa said, "and I was thinking that I'd like to make a chocolate sceptre for the ball. Wouldn't that be so sweet, to walk in holding a royal sceptre?" Cocoa sighed. "I'd be like a fairy princess!"

Just thinking about the sceptre made Cocoa's wings flutter. Even though she was excited about her new strawberry-and-chocolate dot dress with a purple butterfly sweet, she couldn't wait to hold a royal sceptre. "It will be like a magic wand!"

"You will look like a fairy princess," Melli agreed. Then she paused. "Do you know how to make a magic wand?"

Cocoa shook her head. "No, but I plan on learning. I made a sketch of the sceptre that I'd like to make." She held up her drawing. "Did you bring me the caramel ball mould? I wanted

to have a round chocolate sphere at the top."

Melli pulled the round mould out of her bag and gave it to Cocoa. "I was wondering what you were going to do with this," she said.

"I'm meeting Raina later," Cocoa told her. "She's going to lend me a book about magic wands." Carefully, Cocoa folded her drawing up and put the paper back in her bag. "I thought the marshmallow would add a nice touch."

"I think you're right." Melli nodded.

"And I'll need lots of this chocolate," Cocoa added. She took out a pail and dipped it into the pool of chocolate swirling in front of her. "The waterfall chocolate is the best for making special chocolate sweets. I need to hurry home so the chocolate can set. Then I'm going to carve decorations on the ball."

"I can't wait to see that chocolate wand!" Melli cried.

"Thanks," Cocoa replied. She swept up her bucket and headed back to Chocolate Woods. She had lots of work to do before Sun Dip tonight. A chocolate magic wand was no small task. And Cocoa wanted to make sure it was going to be the talk of the Sugar Ball.

2

The Chocolate Sceptre

When Cocoa returned to Chocolate Woods, she poured the fresh chocolate into Melli's hard caramel mould. She knew that she wanted a chocolate ball at the top of her wand—just like the one she had seen in Raina's book. Later, when the chocolate was hard, she would carefully carve the ball with her tools. Oh, she couldn't wait! Her magic sceptre was going to be *choc-o-rific*!

While the chocolate was hardening, Cocoa flew to Gummy Forest to find Raina. Her friend had not one, as promised, but two books on magic wands.

"You should know that it's often sticky business to make magic wands," Raina told her. She pushed her long hair out of her eyes as she spoke. "If wands get into the wrong hands, there can be trouble."

Cocoa laughed. "Oh, chocolate sticks," she said. "It's just for my costume. Raina, you worry too much. And I don't think I am going to let go of it. I've been working so hard on the wand. I'll want to hold my perfect accessory all evening!"

Raina handed the two large books to Cocoa.

"Here you go," she said. "These are two books that have a few different pictures of royal sceptres."

Flipping through the pages, Cocoa's eyes grew wide with excitement. "Oh, this is perfect!" she exclaimed. She noticed the details in the chocolate carvings and the bright colours used for the wands. She had so many ideas, and she wanted to get started right away.

Cocoa felt a gentle nudge and looked down. "Hi, Nokie," she said. Nokie was a little red gummy bear cub. He was always hungry. Even though he didn't eat chocolate, he was hoping that Cocoa might have a treat for him. "I have some fruit chews, if you want," she told him. "Berry gave them to me yesterday, and I'm not going to use them for my hair clips."

Nokie eagerly nodded. Berry had given him fruit chews before and he loved the fruity, sparkly sweets.

"Nokie!" Raina scolded. But she couldn't help smiling at the cute cub when she saw his face. Her voice softened. "Just one, okay?"

The gummy cub quickly agreed and took Cocoa's offering.

"Sorry about that," Raina apologised to Cocoa. "No matter how much I feed Nokie, he's always hungry!"

Cocoa patted the friendly cub on his belly. "It's okay," she said. "I'm happy to share."

"Do you want to see my dress?" Raina asked. "The colour came out perfectly!" She showed her friend the bright lime-green dress with rainbow gummy accents on the waist and hem. She held the gown up to show off the details.

"Oh, Raina," Cocoa gasped. "This is really beautiful. You made this by yourself?"

Raina blushed. "Well, I had some help from Berry. She's so good at designing and sewing. I'm not sure what I would have done without her."

"You are going to look delicious," Cocoa told her. "Have you decided how you'll wear your hair?"

Raina shrugged. "I'm not sure yet," she confided. "Maybe I'll get a fancy updo. What do you think?" She pulled her long, straight hair up and twisted it in a fancy bun. "I could use a rainbow gummy berry for a clip."

"I can't wait to see what you decide," Cocoa told her. "Sure as sugar, every fairy in Sugar

Valley is going to look extra-sweet."

"I know!" Raina exclaimed. "I can't wait!"

Cocoa glanced over at the Frosted Mountains. "I better get going," she said. "I want to carve the chocolate ball before Sun Dip tonight." She winked at Raina. "Maybe I'll bring the wand for a special preview."

"Oh, please do!" Raina pleaded. "I'd love to see what you do." She took Nokie's paw and gave a wave to her friend. "I've got to take Nokie back to his den. I'll see you later."

"Thanks for the books," Cocoa called. She took off and flew swiftly back to Chocolate Woods.

At home Cocoa saw the chocolate in her mould was hard and dry. She selected the smallest pink sugar crystal carving tool for the delicate design

 18

of the chocolate wand. The tiny tool was good for small details. She glanced over at one of the books Raina had given her. She was looking at a couple of different wands and using ideas that she loved about each one. Skillfully she carved a beautiful design on the chocolate ball.

When she finished she stood back and gazed at her sphere. She placed the ball on top of the wand using very hot chocolate and sugar. Then she added a few glittering jewel sweets that she had been saving for a special occasion and a bit of white marshmallow as a finishing touch.

She pointed the wand at a cracker on the table, and instantly it was covered in chocolate.

"Hot chocolate!" she exclaimed. "I really did it!"

The lavender light seeping through her window alerted her to the time. Her friends were probably already gathered for Sun Dip. She took her wand, eager for her friends to see her handiwork.

As she had suspected all her friends were together near the shores of Red Licorice Lake for Sun Dip. Even Berry was there! Berry was hardly ever on time, but she must have been very excited to show off her new fruit-chew jewellery and her ball gown.

"Did you finish your wand?" Melli called out, as soon as she spotted Cocoa.

Cocoa proudly took her prized possession out of her bag. She floated above her friends and waved her royal sceptre. Tiny little pieces of chocolate sprinkled from the wand, and her friends giggled as they grabbed for the sweets.

"So mint!" Dash called out. The little Mint Fairy was the smallest fairy in Sugar Valley, but also one of the fastest. She swooped through the air to gather up the most chocolate. "Cocoa, your wand is beautifu – and *choc-o-rific!*"

"You certainly have a way with chocolate," Melli said.

"Thanks," Cocoa said, grinning. "I can't wait for the ball. We're going to have the best time!"

"And wait till the Sugar Pops see us!" Melli gushed.

"They won't even recognize us," Berry boasted. "The last time we saw them, we weren't in ball gowns. We'd been working in Candy Corn Fields!" She slipped her long gown on over her dress. "Cocoa, will you zip me up?"

"Sure," Cocoa said, setting down the wand. "This gown is *sweet-tacular*!"

Berry twirled around in a circle. The meringue bottom of her dress fell around her in a puffed-out skirt. "I feel like a princess!" she said, beaming.

"And you look like one too," Raina told her. "I think we all will tomorrow night!"

"I better get back home," Cocoa said. She looked up at the sky. The sun was almost behind the Frosted Mountains. "I have to finish my dress." She grabbed her royal wand and put it in her bag. "I'll see you fairies tomorrow!" she cried, as she shot up in the air. "I can't wait for the Sugar Ball!"

3

Chocolate Clues

Speeding through Sugar Valley, Cocoa was
grinning as she thought about the Sugar Ball.
She wondered what Princess Lolli would say
about her wand; after all, she was a *real* fairy
princess. The ruling princess of Candy Kingdom
certainly knew all about royal wands. Cocoa
had long admired the fancy bejewelled sceptre

that Princess Lolli held at important affairs. Her great-grandmother Queen Taffy had passed down the wand to her. It was beautiful and sparkled with the most exquisite rainbow sugar sweets. Cocoa hoped Princess Lolli would be pleased with her chocolate one!

When she arrived home, she put her bag on the chocolate oak table and examined her unfinished dress. She wanted to put a few extra chocolate sprinkles on the waistband.

As she sewed, Cocoa thought about the ball. Sugar Ball was known for elaborate sweets made specially by the Royal Fairies at Candy Castle. Everything at the ball was sugarcoated and delicious! Holding a wand all night might be difficult. If she were to eat any candy, she'd need a free hand. Maybe if she sewed a loop on the side of the dress, she could easily slip the wand in and out.

Cocoa was very pleased with herself. What a *choc-o-rific* idea! She cut some extra fabric and got to work.

The stars twinkled in the dark night sky, and the full moon cast a white glow through Cocoa's window. She'd been hard at work for hours! Cocoa stood back and examined her finished gown. She was so proud of her dress – and the fancy loop on the side of the dress for the wand. Grabbing her chocolate weave bag from the table, she reached inside for her wand to test out her invention.

"Huh?" Cocoa murmured to herself. She stuck her hand into her bag. Where was the wand?

She knew she had put the wand back into her bag before leaving Sun Dip. She never would have left the wand lying on the ground. . .

She searched the bag again. And then she saw her finger poking through a hole at the bottom of her bag. A hole that was big enough for her chocolate wand to fall through!

"Bittersweet chocolate!" she cried.

Cocoa's heart began to race. Her magic wand was gone? Raina's words rang in Cocoa's head. *"If wands get into the wrong hands, there can be trouble."*

The first sour thought that came into Cocoa's head was of the salty old troll Mogu. Mogu lived under the bridge in Black Licorice Swamp and was always on the hunt for Candy Fairy sweets. He had even stolen Cocoa's prized chocolate eggs from their nest in Chocolate

Woods. Cocoa's wings fluttered as she remembered her journey to Black Licorice Swamp with Princess Lolli. The princess had been brave as well as clever, and together, the two fairies had outsmarted that old troll. Would he have tried to steal from her again?

Cocoa rushed outside and called for the sugar flies. She had to get messages to her friends quickly. Sugar flies could be gossips but they were also good for getting messages to friends in a hurry.

Dashing off notes to her friends, Cocoa instructed the flies to deliver the urgent messages. Cocoa knew it was late but she asked her friends to meet her back at Red Licorice Lake. Since that was the last time she'd seen the wand, she figured she would begin her search there.

After the sugar flies took flight, Cocoa flew to the Sun Dip meeting spot. She hoped that on her way she'd spot the wand. Even though the moonlight was bright, Cocoa didn't see any candy jewels glittering on the ground. All that hard work – and all that chocolate magic! Cocoa was melting inside. How could she have been so careless? She should have double-checked her bag!

At Red Licorice Lake, Cocoa took a peppermint light from her pocket. She held the sweet up as she searched the red sugar sand beach.

Not a trace of her wand.

Cocoa sat down on the cool red sugar sand. The valley was dark, and most fairies were home getting ready for bed. Her wings drooped as she thought about having to tell Princess

Lolli her wand had been lost. A magic wand gone missing was not something to take lightly. She'd have to tell her. If Mogu had gotten hold of the wand, there was no telling what would happen! The Sugar Ball would be cancelled. All of Sugar Valley would be in danger. A troll with a magic wand . . . She didn't even want to think about it.

Cocoa pulled her knees up to her chest and buried her head. She hoped that the sugar flies had delivered her messages quickly and that her friends would come soon. Maybe together they'd be able to figure out what to do.

Glancing up, Cocoa saw a thick licorice stalk in front of her. She squinted in the moonlight, unsure of what she was looking at. What was on the top of the stalk? She stood up and flew to the top of the licorice.

It was covered in chocolate syrup!

Someone definitely found the wand here, Cocoa thought. The wand must have fallen out as soon as she took flight! Flying around the stalk, Cocoa wondered why someone would have aimed at the licorice stalk. She floated back down to the ground, searching for more clues. If she followed the chocolate clues, she'd find the wand!

She wasn't sure her plan would work, but she knew one thing. Sure as sugar, she needed all her friends to help her!

CHAPTER 4

Spreading Chocolate

"Cocoa!" Melli cried. She swooped down and knelt near her friend. "Oh, Cocoa, what is going on?" She took a deep breath. "I saw chocolate puddles everywhere as I flew from Caramel Hills!"

Looking up at her friend, Cocoa's lip quivered. She didn't want to burst into tears, so she looked back down at her knees. "My wand . . . ," she began.

Melli's hand was on her back. "Oh, Cocoa. You worked so hard on that wand." And then she took a quick breath as she realised what this news meant. "And now someone has chocolate power!" she gasped.

"Licking lollipops!" Berry blurted out, when she saw her friends. "What is going on here tonight? There's a chocolate explosion around here. You should see Fruit Chew Meadow! Those chews are going to need a power wash to get back to their fruity glory."

"There's chocolate in Fruit Chew Meadow, too?" Cocoa asked. She shook her head. This was worse than she had thought. Someone was definitely using the wand – someone who didn't understand the magic of chocolate.

"Strange," Berry said. She tapped her finger to her chin. "It's like there's a chocolate spell on Sugar Valley or something."

"And that spell is *so mint*!" Dash announced, as she flew in from over the licorice stalks. "These peppermints are delicious with the chocolate sprayed on them. What a minty cool idea." She popped a chocolate-covered sweet in her mouth and then licked her fingers.

"Dash!" Melli scolded. "This isn't a joke. Cocoa's magic wand has been stolen!"

"Not stolen, exactly," Cocoa said sadly. "My wand fell out of my bag when I left Sun Dip." She couldn't keep back her tears anymore. "And now this is all my fault! Raina warned me about making a magic wand."

Cocoa's friends all gasped. A gentle breeze blew and fluttered their wings as the fairies stood in silence.

"Oh, this doesn't look good," Raina said as she joined her friends. She looked at Cocoa. "I came as soon as I got the message. What happened?"

"Please tell me you know a story in the Fairy Code Book about a magic wand that gets into the wrong hands," Cocoa pleaded. She held up her bag and stuck her fingers in the hole. "My wand fell out after I left Sun Dip."

"Hot caramel," Melli muttered. "This is really a sticky situation." Then she realised why Cocoa was so upset. "Do you think Mogu could have picked up the wand?"

"Mogu can't make chocolate," Berry argued. "He's a troll."

"No, but if he is holding a magic wand that was made by a chocolate fairy," Raina said, thinking out loud, "then it might be possible."

Cocoa jumped up from the ground. "What do you mean, *might be possible*?" She grabbed Raina's hand. "You mean in all the stories you've ever read, you've never come across this?" She hung her head. "Oh, this is really bad."

Raina paced back and forth on the red sugar sand. "I don't know," she said. "I'm thinking."

The fairies all watched Raina. They weren't used to seeing her flustered. Raina was always so sure and logical. And usually she could quote a line from the Fairy Code Book that would solve their problem.

"But Raina always knows the answer!" Dash blurted out.

Berry and Melli shot her a look, but Dash just shrugged.

"Raina said it *might* be possible," Berry said. "Maybe there's hope that Mogu couldn't make this chocolate mess."

"That's a chance we can't take," Cocoa said. She stood up. "We need to follow the chocolate trail. Tracking the clues is the only way to find the wand."

Raina nodded. "Cocoa's right. Let's try to figure out where the wand is . . ."

"And who has it," Berry finished for her.

"What if Mogu did take the wand?" Melli asked. She shivered as she thought of the old troll having chocolate power. "What a gooey mess we're in! And right before the Sugar Ball."

"It's my mess," Cocoa said. "I'm going to fly

north toward Candy Castle. From your reports, the chocolate seems to be spreading in that direction."

"You are not going alone," Melli said, standing next to her.

"Sure as sugar, we're all going with you," Raina added.

Dash and Berry nodded. And they all leaned in to hug Cocoa.

"Thank you," Cocoa managed to say. "This means so much to me. I can't bear the thought of facing Princess Lolli with another chocolate mess."

"Don't get your wings stuck in syrup yet," Berry teased. "We can solve this mystery."

Together, the fairies flew to Candy Castle. The pink-and-white sugarcoated castle glistened in the moonlight. The frosted towers and iced tips of the castle looked the same as always. She sighed, relieved that there wasn't a blanket of chocolate covering the castle or the Royal Gardens.

"Doesn't look like there is any chocolate out of place here," Cocoa said.

"Look over there," Raina whispered, pointing. "It's Tula, Princess Lolli's adviser. I wonder what she's doing in the gardens so late at night."

"She's talking to a bunch of Sour Orchard Fairies," Berry said. Berry had once been scared to go to Sour Orchard. She had to find Lemona the Sour Orchard Fairy, who had created the heart-shaped sweets Berry found by Chocolate River. After Berry met her, she found out that those fairies weren't so different from Berry and her friends. Berry squinted her eyes. "I think that might even be Lemona!"

Just then Tula flew into the castle, and Lemona was left standing in the gardens.

"I'm going to ask her what's going on," Berry said. Before Cocoa or the others could react, Berry was at Lemona's side. And then in a flash, Berry was back with news.

"Lemona said that the Sour Orchard was covered in chocolate syrup. Princess Lolli is very concerned about the chocolate mess. She said she'll cancel the Sugar Ball! There can't be a royal celebration when so many parts of the kingdom are under a chocolate spell."

"Oh, this means we're in hot chocolate," Cocoa mumbled. She twisted a strand of her long, dark hair around her finger.

"We need to break this spell immediately!" Berry shouted.

"But first we need to find out who has the wand," Cocoa added quietly.

5

Chocolate Bash

The place Cocoa wanted to check first was Gummy Forest. Raina hadn't seen any chocolate in the forest before she got Cocoa's message, so maybe that was the next place for a chocolate attack. If Cocoa and her friends followed the chocolate, they'd find the wand. And right now Cocoa knew they had to find that wand before all of Sugar Valley was put under a thick, gooey spell!

The moonlight made Gummy Forest look different. Even though Cocoa had been there many times, in the dark the gummy trees and bushes took on spooky shapes. There were chocolate puddles along the ground, and random flowers and berries were chocolate-covered.

Whoever had the wand didn't really know how to handle it—or the magic. The syrupy chocolate was aimed all over the place, and not with a real purpose, the way a Chocolate Fairy would use the wand. Cocoa sighed as she flew through the trees hoping to find her next clue. She had never seen Gummy Forest in such a state. Looking over at Raina, she saw her Gummy Fairy friend was trying to be brave.

"Once we find the wand, I promise to help clean up this mess," Cocoa told Raina. "I am so sorry."

Raina glanced over at Cocoa as they flew. "It's not your fault," Raina said. "The wand falling out of your bag was an accident."

Cocoa lowered her head. She still felt responsible for the chocolate mess.

And then she saw something that made her heart stop.

In a hammock between two large gummy trees, Cocoa spotted Mogu. She froze and put her hand up to alert her friends. The five fairies huddled in the air just above the troll. Mogu was just as Cocoa had remembered him: lying down stuffing his mouth full of chocolate. His hands and face were stained with dark splotches of chocolate, and his large nose was sniffing a chocolate-covered gummy flower. He was making loud slurping sounds as he ate all the chocolate around him.

Cocoa took a deep breath. She tried to summon all the courage that she could. After watching Princess Lolli in Black Licorice Swamp, she knew she had to be brave, as well as clever, to trick this hungry old troll. She motioned for her friends to stay where they were and she got ready to fly down to face Mogu.

Melli grabbed her hand. "Do you want me to go with you?" she asked.

Cocoa shook her head. "No, I need to do this

alone. It's my chocolate wand, and I'm going to get it back."

Her friends all exchanged looks, but they knew that when Cocoa got stuck on an idea, that was the end of the discussion.

"I'll be fine," she said. "I've talked to Mogu before. This time, I know what I need to do. Besides, I know you are right behind me."

"Sure as sugar," Melli said, smiling.

Cocoa flew down to the hammock and took a deep breath.

"Mogu," Cocoa said as she landed next to him. She was surprised at how calm and sure she sounded.

"Ah, the little Chocolate Fairy!" Mogu said. *"Bah-haaaaa,"* he laughed. "I see you have been busy. I love what you've added to this place. I always thought this forest needed a little more chocolate."

Mogu's ring of white hair around his head was sticking up. And his dark, beady eyes were wide with greed. Cocoa tried to steady her breath. She felt as if there was a fire in her belly, heating her up.

Be calm, she thought.

"What are you doing here?" Cocoa asked.

"I'm having an old chocolate bash," Mogu laughed. "What does it look like I'm doing? These chocolate-covered gummy berries are pretty, pretty good." He licked his fingers. *"Bah-ha-ha-haaaaaaa!"*

Cocoa stared at Mogu. He seemed to be on the verge of eating too much chocolate. He didn't look scary. His stomach looked too full of chocolate to allow him to get up. And he had that crazed chocolate gaze in his eyes that she remembered from when she and Princess Lolli had gone to Black Licorice Swamp. He was close to going into a chocolate slumber. Cocoa hoped that wasn't too far off. Then she could search for the wand without his noticing.

"I never would have thought to cover these sweets in chocolate!" Mogu said with a loud burp. He reached his hand down and scooped up a bunch more berries.

Cocoa shot her friends a look. Maybe Mogu was *eating* the chocolate, not *making* the chocolate. She scanned the area and didn't see the wand anywhere. Suddenly Cocoa was encouraged. A lost wand was one thing, but it was another thing if a sour troll had it. And the only thing Mogu seemed to have was a chocolate appetite!

"Maybe you'd like some more chocolate?" Cocoa asked. —

She could tell her friends were confused by her offer, but Cocoa suddenly felt very confident.

"Bah-ha-haaaaaaaa!" Mogu laughed. "I would love that!"

"Well, if you had a magic wand, you could make your own chocolate," Cocoa said. She watched Mogu's face carefully. "You wouldn't need a fairy to make the candy for you."

Mogu stopped eating and stared at Cocoa. "What a big idea from such a small fairy," Mogu muttered. "I want one of those!"

"I bet you would," Cocoa said, smiling. She was so relieved that Mogu didn't have the wand that she touched a gummy flower and gave the

sweet a rich, dark chocolate shell with chocolate sprinkles. "Here," she said. She handed the greedy troll the special treat. "Try this."

Mogu ate the sweet as Cocoa flew up to her friends. "Mogu doesn't have the wand!" she exclaimed.

"Why'd you give him more sweets?" Dash blurted out.

"Because the faster Mogu falls asleep, the sooner he'll stop eating all of Gummy Forest!" Cocoa said, winking at Dash.

"And we've got work to do. We can't spend all day troll-sitting!" Raina said.

Cocoa was thankful to have her friends around her. Together, they would find a way to stop this chocolate spell from spreading all over Sugar Valley.

6

Chocolate Storm

The five fairies watched Mogu sleeping. His mouth fell open, and he began snoring loudly. His chocolate-covered hands dangled off the hammock. With each breath he took, his big belly went up and down. Cocoa was right. The greedy troll's chocolate slumber had begun.

"Now Mogu won't eat all of Gummy Forest!"

Raina declared happily. She sent a sugar fly to Candy Castle with news of Mogu's appearance in the forest. The Royal Fairy Guards would safely fly the sleeping Mogu back to Black Licorice Swamp. The troll would not be eating any more of the Candy Fairies' sweets for a while.

Meanwhile the five friends flew back to Raina's home. They needed a place to think and figure out what to do next.

"Before we start following clues all over Sugar Valley, we need to figure out a plan," Berry said.

Cocoa knew her levelheaded friend was right, but she was anxious to get out and see if there were more chocolate clues. She couldn't help but feel this chocolate mess was all her fault. The faster she found the wand, the faster this would all be over.

"Raina, maybe we should see if anything like this has ever happened in Sugar Valley before," Melli said. "I know you said that you couldn't remember anything in the Fairy Code Book but maybe we can help you look." She glanced over at the wall of books in Raina's room.

"I'm thinking," Raina replied. She was staring at her large bookcase. "There might be something in one of these books." She flew up to the top shelf and then glided back down with three yellow books in her hands. "I remember some kind of chocolate storm. It's barely mentioned in the Fairy Code Book, but maybe the story is in here."

"Why isn't the story in the Fairy Code Book?" Dash asked, peering over her shoulder.

Raina shrugged. "Sometimes there is more to a story than the Fairy Code Book records," she

said. She opened up one of the yellow books. Dust flew from the covers. "Sweet sugar!" she said, blowing away the dust. "I guess I haven't opened this in a while!"

"Are these stories all true?" Cocoa asked.

"I believe that they are," Raina said. "And I think I just found the chocolate storm story!"

Cocoa raced forward to sit next to Raina. All the fairies huddled around as Raina began to tell the story. The way Raina read the story, it felt as if they were all there.

"The sky was filled with dark clouds, and all the fairies in Sugar Valley knew that a winter storm was coming," Raina read. "All the sugar flies were buzzing with the news of terrible weather. Fairies snuggled inside and prepared for the winter storm."

"Yum. I bet they were all drinking hot chocolate with marshmallows!" Dash blurted out. "And the slopes on the Frosted Mountains must have been *so mint*!"

Cocoa smiled at Dash. Even at a time like this, Dash was happy to think about sweets and sledding.

"The snow that fell that day was different from other winter storms," Raina continued to read. "The normal winter white snow that usually fell in Sugar Valley didn't come. Instead, the snow was a deep brown chocolate powder and piled up in high drifts around the valley."

"So they could just make hot chocolate by sticking their cups in the snow!" Dash interrupted.

"Shhh," Melli scolded gently. "Let Raina finish."

Raina looked over at Dash and winked. Then she read more. "The storm lasted for a week. No one knew what to make of the weather. But the fluffy sweet powder was nothing that anyone had ever seen before."

Cocoa leaned over to the book and read the next line with a heavy heart. "Some said it was a gift," she read. "And others said it was a curse. Sugar Valley was under a chocolate spell."

"So mint," Dash said. "I would have had plenty to make out of chocolate snow! Peppermint and chocolate is delicious!"

"The chocolate snow stayed around for weeks," Raina read, turning the page. "Many fairies were cooped up inside their homes. Most fairies learned how to make all sorts of chocolate treats using the powdered chocolate. They had to use the snow. There was so much chocolate!"

"What happened?" Berry asked.

Melli inched forward. She bit her nails. "Go on, Raina," she said. "Tell us what happened."

"The chocolate snow started to melt," Raina said. "There were great chocolate floods and Chocolate River overflowed."

"What a chocolate mess!" Melli muttered.

Raina nodded and continued to read. "The snow seeped into all the sugar soil."

"Oh no," Melli said. "The crops!" Her hand flew to her mouth.

"The spring and summer crops all had a hint of chocolate," Raina read. "It took two whole years to rid the soil of the chocolate taste."

"Bittersweet," Cocoa said, shaking her head. "Too much chocolate is never a good idea."

Berry stood up and walked around. "Do you think the chocolate syrup puddles we saw are going to ruin the crops?"

Melli shot Berry a look.

"What?" Berry said. "I'm just asking."

Cocoa lowered her head. "Berry is asking a good question," she said. She knew that Melli didn't like it when the friends didn't get along, but Cocoa couldn't be mad at Berry for stating the truth. The crops were in danger. This situation was more serious than the Sugar Ball being cancelled. They had to fix this problem quickly before the chocolate spread all over Sugar Valley.

Raina closed the book.

Cocoa sighed. Now what were they going to do?

Chocolate Thoughts

Cocoa fiddled with her chocolate dot bracelet. No one said a word after Raina finished reading the story of the great chocolate storm. Cocoa lifted her eyes from her wrist and glanced at her four friends. Their worried expressions made Cocoa uneasy. The missing chocolate wand could ruin all the sweets in Sugar Valley.

At that moment she almost wished that Mogu had stolen the magic chocolate wand. At least she had some idea how to handle the salty old troll. But now she felt helpless.

Just then Cocoa felt Melli's arm around her. "We need to find the wand, that's all," she said quietly.

"Melli's right," Berry chimed in. "This isn't a huge chocolate snowstorm. Chances are, these chocolate puddles will dry up quickly. The crops will be fine."

"We don't know that," Cocoa whispered.

"Let's see what we do know," Raina said. She took out a notebook and started writing. "There's a missing magic chocolate wand. And chocolate from Sour Orchard all the way to Gummy Forest."

"Someone has definitely gotten hold of the wand. Someone who is clearly not a Chocolate Fairy," Dash said.

Melli flew over to Dash and gave her a tight squeeze. "That's it!" she shouted. "What we need is a Chocolate Fairy to make another wand to clean up the mess! A new magic wand could get rid of the chocolate spell."

"She'd need the first wand to be able to reverse the spell," Raina said, shaking her head.

"But maybe I could make something to help clean up the mess," Cocoa blurted out. "I just can't sit here wondering what to do." She stood up. "Send a sugar fly if you hear or see anything," Cocoa told them. "I'm going back to Chocolate Woods."

"Do you want company?" Melli asked.

Cocoa fluttered her wings. "Maybe in a little while," she said. "For now I need to concentrate on chocolate thoughts."

As Cocoa headed back to Chocolate Woods, she was saddened to see all the puddles of chocolate in Sugar Valley. Berry was right . . . whoever had the wand was not a Chocolate Fairy. A Chocolate Fairy would know how to hold the wand with better aim and skill. She shook her head. But what Candy Fairy would want to steal her wand?

Before Cocoa went into Chocolate Woods, she decided to sit on Caramel Hills to think. She was happy to see that there was no sign of chocolate on the golden hill.

Cocoa sat and wondered what would happen to the crops and thought about how sad all the fairies would be if there was no Sugar Ball. A tear fell from Cocoa's eye. How could she even tell Princess Lolli? To think that she had once been so excited about her chocolate royal wand!

Out of the corner of her eye, Cocoa saw a flash of chocolate. At first she thought she was seeing things. But then she realised – there was a chocolate clue happening right in front of her!

She got up and flew toward the caramel tree dripping with chocolate. She touched the chocolate. The thin chocolate was like syrup.

How strange, she thought. *The wand must be nearby.*

She flew up to the top of the tree and looked around. This had to be a fresh hit. The chocolate hadn't been there before. Her wings began to flutter. Was this the final chocolate clue? She scooted to the edge of the tree branch and scouted the area. She didn't realise it but she was holding her breath. She was nervous and excited at the same time. Right beside a small chocolate oak tree she spotted her chocolate royal wand!

The sight took her breath away and she gasped out loud. Cocoa saw the wand – and knew the fairy holding it!

CHAPTER

8

The Power of Chocolate

Cocoa flew down to the small chocolate oak. Her eyes never left her chocolate wand. "Cara, what are you doing with that?" she asked the small Caramel Fairy. Melli's little sister stood wide-eyed, staring back at her.

"Oh, Cocoa!" Cara cried. Tears sprang from her eyes and she sobbed so hard that Cocoa couldn't understand a word she was saying.

At that moment Cocoa wasn't angry at all. She reached out, took the wand, and put her arm around the young fairy. "Why don't you start at the beginning and tell me what happened?" she asked gently. She guided Cara over to a rock and sat her down.

Cara still hadn't stopped crying. "Please stop," Cocoa begged her. "If we are going to fix this mess, we have to know what happened."

Cara sniffled and took quick breaths to try to calm down. "Please don't tell Melli or Princess Lolli," she said. She looked up at Cocoa. "I really am so sorry for this mess that I've made."

"Cara, just tell me what happened," Cocoa begged. She gave Cara's shoulder a tight squeeze. "I promise I won't be mad."

Cara's shoulders relaxed and she was able to breathe easier. "Well," Cara began, "I saw your wand on the ground after Sun Dip. It was sticking out of one of the licorice bushes by Red Licorice Lake." She wiped her eyes with her hand. "I was going to give it back to you. That's why I picked it up." Her brown eyes glanced at the wand now in Cocoa's hands. "But the wand is just so beautiful."

"It's the power of chocolate," Cocoa said. "It's very hard to resist."

Cara nodded. "Yes," she agreed.

"And so you tried it out?" Cocoa asked.

"I didn't realise the magic was so strong," Cara went on. "As soon as I picked up the wand, things started to change into chocolate." The Caramel Fairy sniffled. "And the more I tried to stop that from happening, the more chocolate I made!"

Standing up, Cara walked over to the chocolate oak and leaned against the tree. "I wanted to fix what I had done but I couldn't," she explained. "I went to find one of Raina's books. I thought I could find the answer without anyone knowing what I had done."

"Why didn't you just come to me or to Melli?" Cocoa asked.

Cara looked down at her golden brown shoes. "I wanted to fix my mess by myself," she said.

"Oh, Cara." Cocoa sighed. "You should never

be scared to tell a friend that you need help."

Pulling her hair away from her face, Cara let out a long sigh. "I guess," she said. "But at the time, I thought Raina's books could offer a quick fix." She let her hair fall around her shoulders.

"Those books don't always have the answer," Cocoa said sadly.

Cara paced around the tree. "When I got to Gummy Forest, Mogu was there!" she said. "I had never seen a troll up close before. He was so salty! I panicked and caused a chocolate explosion."

Cocoa flew over to Cara and took her hand. "Yes, I've seen Gummy Forest." She guided the young fairy back to the rock. "And then why did you go to Sour Orchard?"

"I remember hearing that Berry went to see Lemona the Sour Orchard Fairy," Cara said.

"Lemona was able to help Berry with those sour heart sweets that she found by Chocolate River."

Cocoa remembered how difficult that journey had been for Berry. Berry was afraid to go to a different part of Sugar Valley. Raina had gone with her and together they had found the Sour Orchard Fairy. And Cara, who was much younger, had gone by herself! Poor Cara, she really was trying to do everything alone.

"I didn't get very far into Sour Orchard when the wand starting oozing chocolate syrup," Cara told Cocoa. "Then I knew that I was really in a mess." She hung her head. "I heard the sugar flies buzzing about the Sugar Ball being cancelled, and I got scared. I couldn't believe I had caused so much trouble. I came back here and thought I'd be safe in Chocolate Woods."

The wand in Cocoa's hands sparkled in the sunlight. The jewel sweets were catching the sun's rays and the fairy etched in the round globe was smiling. When she'd had the idea for the Sugar Ball accessory, Cocoa had never dreamed that the wand would create so many problems. Cocoa looked back at Cara's sad face.

"I thought it would be fun to try to be a Chocolate Fairy," Cara said softly. She was staring down at her hands. "At least for a little while."

"Just because you are a Caramel Fairy doesn't mean that you can't work with chocolate," Cocoa told her. "Melli and I work together all the time. But trying to make chocolate? You're going to have to leave that to the Chocolate Fairies."

Cara nodded.

"You know, when I was younger, I really wanted to be a Gummy Fairy," Cocoa told her. "I was so jealous of all the colours that Raina got to play with. Her sweets were all the colours of the rainbow. Chocolate only has a few shades, you know."

"Really? You wanted to be a different kind of fairy?" Cara asked. Her eyes were wide with disbelief.

"Yes, even though I am one hundred percent chocolate!" Cocoa exclaimed. "As you can imagine, my trials didn't work out so well." She laughed to herself as she recalled her attempts. "My sweets were not very good or tasty. I learned an important lesson. Candy Fairies can enjoy all kinds of sweets in Sugar Valley, but when it comes to making sweets, we need to stick with what comes naturally."

Cara giggled. "Well, I believe that. I can't seem to aim right or make anything except chocolate puddles!"

Cocoa was happy to see a smile appear on Cara's face. She held out her hand to her. "Come on," Cocoa said. "Let's let everyone know the wand has been found and get Sugar Valley cleaned up."

For the first time since the wand had disappeared, Cocoa had hope that the Sugar Ball still had a chance of happening.

9

Chocolate Cleanup

Cocoa stood by the chocolate oak tree and watched Cara and Melli. She wanted to give the sisters a few minutes together. After Cara had calmed down, Cocoa pleaded with her to let Melli know what had happened. Just as Cocoa expected, Melli was in Chocolate Woods in a flash once she got the sugar fly message.

Knowing Melli, she would feel terrible that Cara hadn't come to her for help.

Melli's arm was around her sister as the little fairy told her story. After they hugged, Cocoa flew over to them.

"I sent a sugar fly to Candy Castle," she told the sisters. "I wanted to let Princess Lolli know that there was no chocolate spell, just a chocolate mess." She looked at Cara. "I didn't get into all

the details," she said. "So if you want to tell her what happened, that can be your choice."

Cara smiled. "Thank you, Cocoa," she whispered. "And I promise I will tell her. I don't want her to think that any of this was your fault."

"Licking lollipops!" Berry shouted, as she sprang down beside them. "I just heard the sweet news from the sugar flies. No chocolate spell!" She swooped up in the air and then landed on her feet. "But we need a cleanup crew. Sugar Valley is still chocolate-coated."

"And we're just the fairies for the cleanup job," Dash said as she landed next to Berry.

"We came as soon as we heard the good news," Raina added. She hovered above her friends.

Cocoa laughed. "You see, Cara," she said, "you always need your friends around to lend a helping hand."

"Sugar flies really do get the news out in Sugar Valley," Cara said.

"Sure as sugar!" the fairies said together, laughing.

Feeling a boost of energy, Cocoa took charge. "We should each take a part of Sugar Valley to cleanup. The faster we get the chocolate off the ground, the better the chance for the crops."

"And for making sure that the Sugar Ball happens tonight," Melli added.

The fairies all stood together in agreement.

"I'll take Gummy Forest," Raina said.

"Consider Fruit Chew Meadow cleaned," Berry said.

"Peppermint Grove will be chocolate free after I'm done!" Dash exclaimed.

"Cara and I can help out in Sour Orchard," Melli offered. She grabbed her sister's hand and gave it a tight squeeze.

"And I'll take care of Red Licorice Lake," Cocoa added.

"Sounds like we've got a plan," Melli said.

"Hopefully we'll have a Sugar Ball to attend too!" Dash said with a grin. "Now that there is no spell, we can have a party tonight."

"But first we need to make sure all the crops are safe," Cocoa said. "The chocolate puddles haven't been sitting too long, so maybe there won't be any damage."

Raina agreed. "I think we have a good chance," she said. "From what I have read, the chocolate hasn't been on the ground long enough to change the crops."

"Let's all meet back at Candy Castle at Sun Dip," Cocoa told her friends. "That should give us enough time to clean up and then talk to Princess Lolli."

"Oh, I hope she'll let us have the ball," Dash mumbled.

"Me too," Cocoa whispered.

The large orange sun touched the top of the Frosted Mountains. Cocoa was exhausted. Cleaning up after a chocolate mess was not an easy task. Every part of her body ached from the tip of her wings to the bottom of her toes. She looked around at the sugar sand shoreline of Red Licorice Lake. Not a drop of chocolate in sight. Cocoa sighed. She hoped her friends had had the same luck in their spots.

When Cocoa found her friends, they all looked just as worn out as she felt.

"Chocolate cleanup completed," Raina announced when she saw Cocoa. "There was no damage to the gummy crops that I saw."

"Fruit Chew Meadow was fine too," Berry said.

"I think everything is going to be okay," Dash agreed.

Cara stood up. "Melli and I took care of Sour Orchard," she told Cocoa. "Everything looks back to normal."

Cocoa clapped her hands. *"Choc-o-rific!"* she exclaimed.

"I'm going to talk to Princess Lolli," Cara said.

Cocoa and her friends surrounded Cara.

Princess Lolli was fair and true, but telling her something like this would be scary for the young fairy.

"We'll go with you," Cocoa told her. She knew she was speaking for all her friends.

The fairies found Princess Lolli in the royal throne room. She listened to Cara's story about finding Cocoa's wand and how she couldn't stop the chocolate from spreading all over Sugar Valley.

"I am in favour of the fairies experimenting with new sweets and techniques," Princess Lolli said, "but you should always ask permission. Especially if magic is involved."

Cara nodded her head. "I promise never to try that trick again," she vowed. "From now on, I'm sticking with caramel."

"A fine choice for you," Princess Lolli told her. "You are a good Caramel Fairy, Cara. You are full of sweetness and I know you didn't mean any harm to the kingdom."

Melli took Cara's hand. "Please don't ever feel that you can't come to me for help."

"All of us are here for you," Cocoa said. "Sure as sugar."

Cara smiled as she looked at the fairies around her. "Thank you," she said. "I promise."

Princess Lolli glanced up at the large clock on the wall. "Sun Dip is over, and now it's getting late." She turned to look at the other fairies. "What do you think about getting on with the Sugar Ball?"

The fairies all cheered.

"Those are some extra-sweet words!" Cocoa

cried. "I can't wait to wear my new dress." She put her hands on her hips. "But maybe I should leave my chocolate wand at home."

Everyone laughed but Princess Lolli shook her head.

"You've worked very hard on that wand, Cocoa," the fairy princess said. "Please don't leave the wand at home."

Cocoa's wings fluttered and she couldn't help but smile. "I would love to bring my chocolate wand tonight. And I won't be letting it out of my sight for the whole night!"

CHAPTER 10

Chocolate Dip

The grand ballroom at Candy Castle was glorious. The entire room was glowing with tiny sparkling white sugar lights. Each table was covered with a white tablecloth with tall sugar blossom branches in brightly coloured gummy vases. The tiny white flowers on the branches were shimmering with coloured sugar.

The room had never looked so sweet.

Cocoa twirled around in a circle in front of her friends.

"The dress is delicious," Berry remarked.

Blushing, Cocoa smoothed out the skirt. "Thank you," she said. "A comment like that from you is extra-sweet."

Across the room Cocoa saw Cara. She was wearing a short dark caramel dress with a sparkling tiara in her hair. Cocoa flew over to her and noticed that the sweet tiara was covered in tiny caramel drops.

"Your tiara is extraordinary," Cocoa told her.

Cara curtsied. "Thank you. I may not be able to handle chocolate but I am learning how to make caramel!"

"Well done," Cocoa cheered.

Princess Lolli came over to Cocoa and Cara. Her pink-and-white-sugar layered dress looked scrumptious. In her left hand, Cocoa noticed the royal wand. Princess Lolli's wand was made entirely of sugar crystals. The wand was dazzling with the sugar-frosted jewels. Cocoa couldn't take her eyes off it.

"I see you did bring your chocolate wand," Princess Lolli said to Cocoa. "I'm glad that you did. Your work is excellent. You should be proud."

"Thank you," Cocoa said. "And I'm not letting the wand go!" She laughed. "No more crazy chocolate episodes in Sugar Valley."

"Let's hope not," Princess Lolli said, grinning.

Cara held her hand up to her chest. "Certainly not from me," she vowed.

Princess Lolli winked at her. "Enjoy the party,"

she said, as she flew to greet more guests.

"Look," Melli cried, as she raced over to Cara and Cocoa. "It's the Sugar Pops! They really are here!" She pointed to the far corner of the room, where a stage was set up.

"Where are the Sugar Pops?" Dash and Berry exclaimed from behind Melli. She looked all around.

Raina landed next to Dash. "The Sugar Pops are here already?" she asked.

Melli laughed. "They are right there," she said. She put her hands on their shoulders and faced them in the right direction.

Once everyone saw the brothers they let out a sigh.

"Now the party can really begin," Cocoa said, smiling.

"Char is just so yummy," Melli said with a sigh. "Look at that hat. He is just the sweetest."

Dash flew up above her friends to get a better view. "I don't know," she said. "I think Chip is just delish."

Cocoa laughed. "Well, together those three have the best sound in Sugar Valley. Let's go say hi to them."

Melli pulled at Cocoa's hand. "Do you think they will remember us?" she asked.

"Hot chocolate!" Cocoa exclaimed. "Of course they will remember! How could they forget the fairies who saved Caramel Moon?"

The four friends laughed and followed Cocoa over to the front of the stage.

Just as Char, Carob, and Chip took centre stage, Cocoa caught Char's eye. He grinned down at her and then whispered in his brothers' ears.

A hush fell over the crowd. Everyone wondered what the Sugar Pops were up to. Char grabbed the microphone and greeted the crowd.

"Hello, Candy Kingdom!" he sang out. "Happy Sugar Ball! We're so happy to be here today now that the chocolate mess has ended." A roar of cheers and applause echoed in the room. "And we'd like to call up five of our fairy friends to help us with our first song, 'Chocolate Dip.'"

"'Chocolate Dip' is my favorite song!" Cocoa exclaimed. She grabbed her friends and they all flew to the stage. They were so excited to be close to the famous singers again. Cocoa reached out and took Cara's hand. "Come with us!" she shouted.

Char nodded and the music started. The

friends huddled together and swayed to the music. Looking out at the crowd, Cocoa saw that everyone was having a great time. She waved her wand at the end of the song and tiny chocolates fell around the Sugar Pops. The boys laughed and threw the sweets out in the crowd.

"Nice touch, Cocoa," Char whispered. "That is some wand!"

Cocoa thought her heart would melt!

"Oh, you have no idea," Melli mumbled. Laughing, Melli gave Cocoa a tight hug.

The Sugar Pops went on to play all their hits. All the fairies in the kingdom were rocking out to their sweet sounds. The Sugar Ball was a great success and everyone was having a supersweet time.

Cocoa went over to Cara and put a chocolate

drop in her hand. "If you ever need any chocolate, please never hesitate to ask me," she said.

"Don't worry," Cara told her. "I know where to find my chocolate. You have my word that I will be more responsible."

"Sure as sugar," Cocoa said. "This is the best Sugar Ball ever!"

She twirled Cara out on the dance floor. "Maybe we can work on some caramel and chocolate sweets together."

"I would love that," Cara said, smiling.

"Me too," Melli said, coming between them. "Count me in."

"Count us all in!" Dash exclaimed.

"The more fairy friends, the sweeter!" Cocoa announced. And then she fluttered her wings and spun around to the music.

FIND OUT

WHAT HAPPENS IN

A Valentine's Surprise

Raina the Gummy Fairy sprinkled handfuls of colourful flavour flakes into Gummy Lake. She smiled as the gummy fish swam over and gobbled up the food. Watching the fish eat made Raina's tummy rumble. She had gotten up very early and had been working in Gummy Forest all morning. When she settled on a perch high up on a gummy tree, Raina opened her backpack. All the animals in the forest were fed, and now she could relax and eat her own lunch.

Raina had an important job in Sugar Valley. She took care of the gummy animals that lived in Gummy Forest. There were many types of gummy animals, from friendly bear cubs to playful bunnies. Raina was fair and kind to each of the animals – and they all loved her.

"Hi, Raina!" a voice called out.

Raina looked up to see Dash, a Mint Fairy, flying in circles above her head. The small, sweet fairy glided down to see her.

"I was hoping to find you here," Dash said. "I need your help."

Raina was always willing to help out any of her friends. She had a heart that was pure sugar. "What's going on?" she asked.

Dash landed on the branch next to Raina. She peered over at the bowl in Raina's hand. Dash was small but she always had a huge appetite!

"Hmmm, that smells good," she said. "What is that?"

"It's fruit nectar. Berry brought me some yesterday," Raina told her. She watched Dash's eyes grow wider. It wasn't hard to tell that Dash would love a taste. "Do you want to try some?" she asked.

"Thanks," Dash said, licking her lips. "Berry's nectars are always supersweet." Dash leaned over for her taste. Berry the Fruit Fairy had a flair for the fabulous. And she could whip up a spectacular nectar. "Yum," Dash continued. "Berry makes the best fruit nectar soup."

Raina laughed. "I don't think I've ever heard you say that you didn't like something a Candy Fairy made," she told her minty friend.

"Very funny," Dash said, knowing that her friend was speaking the truth.

"Have you come up with any ideas about what to get Berry?" Raina asked.

Dash flapped her wings. "That is why I'm coming to see you," she said. "I was hoping you could give me an idea. I know Berry would love something from Meringue Island but that is a little too far. She's the only one I haven't gotten a gift for and Valentine's Day is tomorrow. Since it's also her birthday, I want to make sure the gift is supersweet."

"Sure as sugar, Berry would love anything from Meringue Island," Raina agreed. Meringue

Island was in the Vanilla Sea and was *the* place for fashion. Berry loved fashion – especially jewellery and fancy clothes. When Fruli, a Fruit Fairy, had come to Sugar Valley from the island, Berry was very jealous of her. Fruli had beautiful clothes and knew how to put together high-fashion looks.

"The truth is," Raina added, leaning in closer to Dash. "Berry would like anything you gave her."

"But I want to give her something she is really going to love," Dash replied. She swung her legs back and forth. "I want to surprise her with a special gift this year." Her silver wings flapped quickly. "I wish I could think of something with extra sugar!"

"I know how you feel," Raina said. "I've had the hardest time coming up with an idea." She looked over at Dash. "I'll tell you what I'm going to get her but please keep it a secret."

"Sure as sugar!" Dash exclaimed. She clapped her hands. "Oh, what are you planning?"

Raina took her last sip of the fruit nectar. "Last night I was reading a story in the Fairy Code Book and I got a delicious idea."

Dash rolled her eyes. "I should have guessed that this would have something to do with the Fairy Code Book," she said.

Raina read the Fairy Code Book so often that her friends teased her that she knew the whole book by heart.

"Well," Raina continued, "there is a great story in the book about Lyra, the Fruit Chew Meadow unicorn."

"Oh, I love Lyra," Dash sang out. "She grows

those gorgeous flower sweets at the edge of the meadow." Just as she said those words, Dash knew why Raina's grin was so wide. "You talked to Lyra and she is going to give you a special flower for Berry?"

Raina laughed. "Dash!" she said. "You ruined my surprise." She put her empty bowl back inside her bag. "I thought that if I got Berry a flower, I could make a headband for her. You know how she loves to accessorise."

"The more the better, for Berry," Dash added. "And those are the fanciest flowers in the kingdom. *So mint!* Berry is going to love that headband." Dash stopped talking for a moment to take in the whole idea. "Wait, how'd you get Lyra to do that for you? Unicorns don't like to talk to anyone!"

Raina smiled. "Well, that's not really true," she said.

"Let me guess," Dash said. "Did you read that in a book?"

Raina giggled. "Actually, I didn't," she told her friend. "To be honest, I think Lyra is just shy."

"Really?" Dash asked. "Can I meet her? Maybe she'll have another idea for a gift for Berry. Let's go now." She stood up and leaped off the branch into the air.

"I've been working all morning," Raina said. She reached her arms up into a wide stretch. "Maybe we can go in a little while?"

Dash fluttered back down to the branch. Her small silver wings flapped quickly. "Come on," she begged. "Let's go now!"

Dash was known for being fast on the

slopes of the Frosted Mountains – and for being impatient. She liked to move quickly and make fast decisions.

Leaning back on the gummy tree, Raina closed her eyes. "Please just let me rest a little and then we can go," she said with a yawn.

"All right," Dash said. "Do you have any more of that nectar?"

Raina gave Dash her bowl and poured out some more of Berry's nectar. Then she shut her eyes. Before Raina drifted off to sleep, she imagined Berry's happy face when she saw her birthday present. Sure as sugar, Valentine's Day was going to be supersweet!

Candy Fairies

Read all the books
in the Candy Fairies series!